Ant God

by

James Lovegrove

First published in 2005 in Great Britain by
Barrington Stoke Ltd, Sandeman House, Trunk's Close,
55 High Street, Edinburgh EH1 1SR
www.barringtonstoke.co.uk

ISBN 1-842993-29-1

Printed in Great Britain by Bell & Bain Ltd

A Note from the Author

There are two main people in *Ant God*. Dan, who's telling the story, and Jason Finnegan.

Jason is a clever boy who's always thinking up amazing ideas.

But he's a bit of a weirdo. He doesn't have many friends and lives in his own world a lot of the time. He "dances to the beat of a different drum", as the saying goes.

Maybe you know some kids a bit like that? I did when I was at school. In secret, I admired them for the way they were. They did their own thing and didn't seem to care what everyone else thought of them. They didn't try to be cool and fit in with the "right" crowd.

I think now that I should have been brave and tried to make friends with them.

I'm glad that I never knew someone who was *exactly* like Jason. I'm even gladder that I never became friends with someone *exactly* like him. But Dan, who tells this story, *was* Jason's friend and it wasn't easy. You're going to find out why.

Ant God is dedicated to all at
Barrington Stoke

Contents

Chapter 1

Jason and Me

This is the story of what happened with Jason and me.

It's the first time I've told the story this way. It'll be the last time, too.

This isn't what I told the police. This isn't what I told Jason's parents or mine. This isn't what I told anyone at school who asked.

The way I told the story to those people was close to the truth but it wasn't the whole truth. It was like a photocopy or a picture you send on a mobile phone. My story was a bit fuzzy and blurred. It made sense and looked almost like the real thing, but it wasn't *all* the story. Bits were missing.

I left out the bit about the ants' nest. I didn't tell anyone about the Truth Glasses. And I didn't tell them about the *thing* I saw through the Truth Glasses, or thought I saw.

I left out bits because other people wouldn't know that they were missing. But, most of all, I left them out because there's some stuff no-one would believe or would want to believe.

It's stuff I don't want to believe myself.

Here it is anyway, just this once – the real story, every bit of the story, the whole truth.

What happened with Jason and me was this ...

Chapter 2

The Ants

We were burning ants with a magnifying glass one afternoon at Jason's house. Jason found it lying on the Yellow Pages. His mum had been using it to see the tiny print better.

It was Jason's idea to take it outside. The magnifying glass was Jason's. We were bored and it was hot. Summer was coming to an end. All the lawns in the city were brown and the leaves on the trees were crisp and ready to drop off.

We were out in the garden and Jason showed me where a line of ants was crossing part of the patio.

The ants were moving in two lines. One lot was going towards the house, the other lot towards the grass.

"Have you seen how every so often two of them stop and chat?" Jason said. "Their antennae touch and then the ants move on. They're just like people meeting in the street. 'Hi. How are you?' 'I'm fine, thanks. How are you?'"

He was right. I had seen ants do this before but I'd never thought of it as chatting.

"They're passing on messages to each other," Jason went on. "They're telling each other to keep going. Or they're saying, 'There's food this way. We must be getting it back to the nest.' Things like that."

I was sure that what he was saying about the messages was true. Jason was very smart, almost too smart for his own good.

"Yeah, just like people meeting in the street," he said.

Then with a sudden horrid grin he said, "Let's burn them."

He picked up the magnifying glass. He held it up to the sun. A beam of sunlight shone through the lens and Jason pointed it like a laser onto the line of ants.

The ants scurried fast. At first Jason couldn't keep the bright pinprick of sunlight fixed on any of them long enough for anything to happen. But he soon got good at it.

He would choose an ant and aim at it. After a few seconds the ant would stop and look confused. Its body would try to get away from the light but it would be unable to escape. It was as if its feet were stuck to the ground. The ant would roll over and start to shrivel and curl in on itself. In next to no time it was just a little feathery black dot on the patio brickwork, not moving.

Jason killed about 20 ants in this way. Each died in a bright white beam of light. I don't think the ants understood what was happening to them. Could such tiny insects feel pain? I hoped not.

Then Jason passed me the magnifying glass and said, "Have a go." I said no. He made me do it. I took the magnifying glass and tried to copy him. But I hated it so I didn't try very hard. Anyway, I couldn't focus the sunlight.

"Wimp," said Jason.

"See that?" I said, as I put down the magnifying glass. I pointed at the ants. "They're carrying off the dead ones."

Jason peered down. They were. Several living ants had come round each of the dead ones. They touched the dead ant with their antennae, ran in small circles, then touched it again. After a few moments, pairs of them picked up the dead ants and the others went on marching to-and-fro. The pairs of ants carried the dead bodies off towards the grass. I think they were taking the dead ants back to the nest to bury them. It was all very clever and tidy.

"Just like people," Jason said, for the third time. He smiled.

Then, all at once, he stood up and started stamping his feet.

"Earthquake!" he yelled. "Earthquake!"

The ants went into a panic. Their tidy, to-and-fro lines broke up and it was every ant for itself. They swirled and scattered, hurrying in all directions. Some of them got squashed under Jason's trainers. The rest vanished. They must have rushed to safety somewhere.

Jason sniggered. Jason laughed.

He stopped stamping.

"Earthquake's over. What a natural disaster. They'll be telling their queen about it back at the nest. 'It must have been a very big quake, your majesty, at least eight point five on the Richter scale.'"

"Jason, you know, sometimes you are a very weird person."

"Oh, I know." Jason gave a happy nod. "But you're my friend, Dan, so if I'm weird, what does that make you?"

I sighed. "You're right. Even weirder."

Jason looked hard down at the ground. There wasn't an ant anywhere, apart from what was left of the ones who'd been crushed under his feet.

Jason was frowning, and I knew what that look meant. He was having some deep and meaningful thought. There was a Big Idea growing in his brain.

Jason couldn't help himself. He was full of Big Ideas.

"I've had a Big Idea," he said. His eyes were far-away, but I knew he was thinking about something that was deep in his mind.

I sat back down on the lawn. "Go on, then. What is it?"

"No. Tonight. I'll ring you tonight, when I've thought about it some more. You go home now, Dan. I've got to get off up to my room to think. See you."

Without another word he went indoors. I was left in the garden on my own, feeling foolish and a bit fed up. Jason had done this to me before, a few times. It was just how he was, and I should have been used to it.

But whenever he left me on my own like that, I always felt as if his Big Ideas were the only thing that mattered to him. He didn't think anything else was important, not even his one and only real friend, me. I was useful to have around, I was someone to hang about with and talk to, but in the end, all Jason really cared about was what was going on inside his own head.

But I still wanted to know what he was thinking about. As I set off home, I was longing to find out what Big Idea he had come up with this time.

Chapter 3

The Railway Cutting

Jason's house and mine were on two sides of a railway cutting. The railway was the main line which ran through the suburbs where we lived and right into the middle of the city. There were two sets of tracks, and about six trains came by both ways, every hour.

During the rush hour there were about ten an hour. I've always lived in this house, so the clattering, rumbling swish of the trains was something I didn't notice. I never heard the trains unless I was listening out for them. I didn't even notice the trains' horns, even though the drivers often honked in greeting if they knew each other.

The houses on Jason's street and on mine had long back gardens. There were trees and bushes at the ends of the gardens as well, so you could hardly see the railway line at all from the house.

The banks of the cutting were steep and covered with brambles and thorn bushes. Each garden had a fence at the end to stop people getting onto the tracks. But with all the trees and shrubs and the thorn bushes you could hardly get through onto the railway line anyway. Most of the fences had been left to rot and fall down and were hidden under all the greenery. Nature had done a good job of stopping you getting out onto the railway.

Of course, Jason and I felt that the best way to get to each other's house was the shortest way.

It was also the most dangerous way. Our parents thought we would use the safe, sensible route, but that meant a long round trip. Each of us would have to go up the street to the junction at the end, over the road bridge across the railway and down the street on the other side. It was nearly a kilometre that way. If you went the short way, from one garden to the other, down the back and across the tracks, that was less than 100 metres.

Of course we never told our parents we did this. We had a clever way of tricking them. If I was going to Jason's, I'd ring him to say I was coming. Then I'd pretend to leave by the front door but in fact I'd sneak out by the back door. Then I would cross the tracks and Jason would let me in secretly at the back of his house. A bit later, he'd make a lot of noise and open the front door as if I'd just arrived there. When he came to see me, I'd do the same for him.

It worked fine. I don't think our parents ever knew what was really going on.

The afternoon that we'd watched the ants, I went home the quick way. Jason's mum and dad were out so I didn't have to make a show of pretending to leave by the front door. I fought through the bushes at the end of his garden, slipped through a gap in the fence, and slid-skidded down the bank of the cutting. The brambles and thorn bushes were thick, and sometimes I had to push branches aside with my arm, a bit like an explorer in the jungle.

Then I was by the tracks and standing on the chunky grey gravel.

I checked both ways, looking and listening as best I could. I could see more than a kilometre down the tracks both ways and the tracks were empty. There were no trains coming. Still, you could never be too sure. They went fast, those trains. One moment there'd be nothing there. Next moment, a city express train could be hurtling towards you.

I stepped across the tracks. I trod on the wooden sleepers and kept off all the rails, not just the electrified ones. With a few quick leaps I got across to the other side.

My heart was thudding just that little bit harder than normal. I always felt scared, no matter how many times I crossed that railway line. Perhaps that was a good thing. I knew that if I ever became careless or relaxed as I crossed the line, I could very well end up dead.

I clambered up the bank to my garden. There was lots of ivy underfoot, trying to trip me up. There were nettles as well, trying to sting me.

I climbed over the broken fence at the top. I checked to make sure that the garden was empty and nobody was looking out of a window.

It was OK. I set off across the garden to the back door.

I was home, safe and sound.

It was only then that I could allow myself to start thinking again about Jason's latest Big Idea.

Perhaps it had something to do with the ants and that earthquake he had made by stamping on their nest?

But what? What had lit up a bulb in that strange, busy mind of Jason's?

I would find out that night.

Chapter 4
The Big Idea

Jason rang that evening as he'd said he would.

All through dinner I'd been thinking about some of the other Big Ideas he'd had. I remembered how once he'd made up his mind that the names for the stars in the night sky were wrong. He didn't think the pictures that people made from the patterns of the stars were right. They made dot-to-dot drawings of the stars they saw and gave them names – Orion the Hunter, the Great Bear, Cancer the Crab and so on. Jason joined the dots in a different way. He called these new patterns things like Dennis the Office Worker, Bobby Bicycle, the Three Frogs, and A Random Squiggle Which Looks Quite Like the Incredible Hulk.

Then there was the time Jason decided that cats ruled the world. We humans were their slaves. We did everything the cats wanted, without even being told to. We fed them, stroked them and gave them somewhere warm and cosy to sleep. When you saw a cat sitting on a wall, it wasn't just having a nap or looking around lazily. The cat was a spy. It was watching to make sure all us humans were good slaves and doing what the cats wanted us to do.

Yet another Big Idea of Jason's was that every city was alive. The electricity that ran through it in cables was like our nervous system. The water pipes and sewers were its digestive system. The roads that took people and traffic into the city and out of it were the veins carrying blood. Jason even made something from an old radio and a brand new portable CD player. He said it was a machine to record the thoughts of our own city. He said it worked really well, but all I heard when I listened to it was a lot of hiss and what sounded like mixed-up radio station signals.

There had been loads of other Big Ideas. Some were madder than others. All were different and strange and you could *almost* believe in them.

They didn't bother me anymore. I knew they were crazy, but in a strange way I looked forward to each new one.

Jason rang me on my mobile from his mobile. We had our own ringtones, so I knew when it was him calling before I even picked up the phone.

"Yeah?" I said.

"You at your window?" Jason said.

"Hang on a sec. OK, I'm there."

I opened my bedroom curtains. It was late, nearly 10 p.m., but not fully dark yet. The sky above the city was a deep, smoky blue. I peered out through the trees, across the railway cutting, to where Jason's house was. His bedroom was at the back like mine. The light from his window was a yellow rectangle and he was like a small, black shape framed in the middle of it. I must have looked exactly the same to him.

"Right, this is it," Jason said. "This is my Big Idea. Remember the ants this afternoon?"

"What ants?" I said with a smirk.

"Don't be silly. And you remember how we were standing there for a bit on the patio and they were totally ignoring us?"

"They didn't ignore us once you started frying them."

"Yeah, but before that. Even when our shadows were on them, they just kept plodding along like we weren't there."

"Maybe they couldn't see us."

"Exactly, Dan! Exactly! They couldn't see us. And d'you know why? It's because we were too big. We were enormous to them. Their tiny eyes and brains couldn't cope with something as big as us, so they just didn't see us. We were too big for them to understand – on a scale they could not comprehend."

"'A scale they could not comprehend.' You watch much too much of the Sci-Fi Channel, Jason."

"Just listen to me, Dan. Hear me out. So the ants couldn't see us, but as soon as we started killing them, they noticed."

"*You* started killing them. Not me."

Jason carried on as if I hadn't said anything. "They noticed. As soon as we started messing up their lives, they knew we were there. Or they knew *something* was there anyway. Something was burning them from above. Something made that earthquake happen and made them rush about like crazy."

"And that something is a cruel teenage kid who's a bit of a psycho."

"That something, Dan, is a god," said Jason.

I held the phone away from my ear and shook it as if there was a problem with it, as if the signal had gone. Jason just might have been able to see me do this, from his window.

"A god?" I said. "What are you talking about? You're telling me you're a god?"

"Not quite. What I'm saying is, to those ants I was a god. Think about it. They couldn't see me, they didn't know I existed, but then a few of them died and they didn't know why. Then there was a huge

22

earthquake that rocked their world. You know what people call earthquakes, and tidal waves, and tornadoes, and other natural disasters that kill lots of people? They call them 'Acts of God', don't they? And in church the vicars are always saying that God is invisible. God cannot be seen. He's there, He's everywhere, but we can't see Him. He's too huge, too powerful, for us to understand. He's all around us but we can only be sure He's there when He affects our lives. When He makes someone very ill so that they're going to die. Or when He makes someone's car crash."

"God doesn't do that. Bad driving does that."

"Does it? How do you know? How can you be sure?"

He had me there. I couldn't be sure. My parents didn't believe in God or anything and nor did I. And yet I felt that there must be some kind of god up there, watching over everyone. There had to be a god with some kind of plan for us all. Or what was the point of anything?

I didn't like to think that a god could be a teenage boy. I didn't fancy being bossed around by a Supreme Being who was as crazy as Jason Finnegan. Someone who kept having Big Ideas and doing odd things.

"You don't believe me, do you?" Jason said.

At least he'd got that bit right.

"Not to worry," he went on. "You will. I already know what to do. Give me a few days. Then I'll show you. You'll see. This is my biggest Big Idea yet, Dan. This is the one I've been working towards all my life. I think it could really make a difference. It could even change the world."

"If you think so, Jason."

"I *know* so, Dan."

I ended the call with a click of a button and I saw Jason do the same thing on the other side of the tracks.

The glowing yellow rectangle of his window vanished as he drew his curtains shut.

I drew mine shut and settled down to sleep.

Chapter 5
The Truth Glasses

It was three days before I heard from Jason again. He kept his mobile switched off. If I couldn't ring him to say I was coming over to visit, I couldn't go over to his house.

This normally happened when Jason had a Big Idea. There might be a few days while he worked on it. Sometimes he would be making a machine or writing a report to show the Idea was real, or else that it was all wrong. Other times he would come and see me the next day and act as if nothing had happened, as if he hadn't had any Big Idea at all.

Most of his Big Ideas ended up that way. He would forget about them. In the end, even the ones he'd spent days working on got forgotten too. He said they were "on hold" and he would return to them sometime, but he never did.

I hoped that this time the Big Idea would be forgotten about fast. I didn't like what Jason thought about God. I wished he'd never come up with the idea.

But there he was, three days later, in my bedroom with a very weird thing in his hands.

It looked a bit like a pair of glasses. There were sticking-out arms that went over your ears. A piece of metal at the front was shaped like an upside-down U and fitted over your nose.

But those were the only parts that looked like normal glasses.

Instead of a right-hand lens, there was a short bit of copper pipe. It was the sort of pipe that plumbers use for radiators and boilers. On the end of that Jason had put the lens from a microscope. And on the end of *that* were two small thin metal needles. They were stuck on across each other. They were the marks you see when you look down a gun and aim it.

For a left-hand lens, Jason had used the bottom of a clear plastic Coca-Cola bottle. Over this he'd stuck a piece of red glass and a piece of green glass. He said both pieces came from a stained-glass window in a church. *How could they have?* I think they came from some other coloured bottles. The bits overlapped, and where they did there was a jagged brown line that ran down between them.

To add to all this, the "glasses" had a third lens.

It sat above the other two, in the middle. This third lens was made from some fuse wire which had been bent into a circle. Over the top of the circle was some Clingfilm. Jason had glued jewels onto the Clingfilm. They weren't real jewels, of course. They were the fake plastic sort that little girls play with.

"I call them Truth Glasses," Jason said in a solemn voice. "They show you the things you can't see in normal life. They show the truth. Things that our brains can't take in."

"Oh yeah?" I said.

"Oh yes," Jason replied, firmly. "I made the glasses so that they could show me one thing most of all."

"And what's that?"

"What do you think? God, of course."

"Oh." For a moment I didn't know what to say. In the end, I said, "Well, have you tried them on?"

"I have."

"And what did you see?"

He took a while to answer. "It was incredible. I mean it, Dan. What it was ... The size of it! The shape of it! It was horrible and yet also amazing."

Jason was sounding weirder than normal when he said this. His voice had a hollow tone to it. He sounded like someone in a movie who has taken drugs. I thought he must be putting it on.

"Really?" I said.

"You should try them yourself, Dan. It'll blow your mind. Wait till dark, though. They work better at night."

Chapter 6
What I Didn't See

I didn't want to try out the Truth Glasses. On the first night the sky was cloudy and overcast. I thought it would be better to try them on a clear night.

The next night, the sky was clear, but I still didn't want to give the glasses a go. There was something about them. They sat on the desk in my bedroom. I felt as if they were watching me. It was as if they wanted me to put them on, and that made me *not* want to.

The biggest problem with them, for me, was that third lens. Jason had told me that there is a part of the brain just behind the forehead. It's some sort of gland and it's kind of a left-over part of the optic nerves – the nerves that control your eyes. I remember a biology teacher once talked about this in a lesson. The teacher said the gland didn't do anything. It's like your appendix in your guts, something which isn't needed in your body any more. It's left over from when we were cavemen.

But Jason said that gland *was* meant for something. It was what some people called the *Third Eye*. It was an eye that could see spirits and the invisible worlds of the dead, if you knew how to look with it.

The third lens on the Truth Glasses was for the Third Eye. The jewels worked a bit like one of those tubes you shake, full of shapes and colours. With this third lens, your Third Eye would be able to see things it had never seen before. That's what Jason said.

That was another thing that made me *not* want to try the glasses on. If it was something I shouldn't see, then it was better that it stayed that way.

Jason rang a few times. As it was his special ringtone, I didn't pick up. He left voicemail messages. Each time he asked if I'd used the glasses yet. The fact that I didn't call back must have given him his answer. Soon he stopped ringing.

In the end, on the third night, I thought, *What the hell.* Jason was a nutter. I knew that. I'd always known that. His Truth Glasses were nothing more than a lot of old bits and pieces all knocked together. I wouldn't see anything through them that I couldn't see anyway. Perhaps I wouldn't see anything at all.

The night was warm and still and cloudless. There were even stars in the sky, which you don't often get in the city.

I switched the bedroom lights off and opened the window wide. I leaned out with the Truth Glasses in my hand. I waited a moment, then I lifted them up and put them on.

At first, just as I'd thought, I couldn't see anything. There were a few dim points of light. They must have been windows or streetlamps. Apart from that, everything was a blur, and black.

I peered hard. I was sure now that I wouldn't see anything new. Nothing the glasses could show me would turn me into a headcase like Jason.

After a time, I got used to the glasses and I saw more.

My right eye seemed to be looking down a long tunnel. At the far end there was the cross-shape of the two needles. I could just make them out because they glinted a bit.

My left eye saw mixed-up patterns and spots of bright colour. At the centre, where the red and green glass overlapped, there was a blank strip.

And what about my Third Eye?

Well, if I said I saw anything at all with it, it would be a lie.

At least, I don't *think* I saw anything.

Just as I was about to take the glasses off, I thought I saw a shape. Somewhere up high, there was movement. I thought I saw an enormous outline which shimmered for a second and blotted out the stars. I tried to focus on it through the glasses, but as I did, the shape vanished.

I pushed the glasses off. My eyes went all blurry. I had been wearing the glasses for 15 minutes. My eyes took a few seconds to see properly again. My nose felt sore where the glasses had been.

I blinked and peered up. What had I seen in the sky? Was it a low-flying jumbo jet, or a cloud, something like that?

I looked up. I couldn't see any jet or cloud. There was nothing but the sky and the stars.

Then I heard a far-away hiss that grew quickly to a rumble. A train sped past the bottom of the garden. It came and went in a matter of seconds. It had four coaches. The 22.47 train out of the city, the second-to-last train of the day.

The tracks whined as the train moved past. Then all was silent again.

I thought about putting the glasses back on and trying to look for that huge shape I had seen or *thought* I had seen.

I decided not to.

I closed the curtains. First I put the glasses back on the desk.

Then, to be extra safe, I put the glasses away in a drawer.

That way they couldn't stare at me while I slept.

Chapter 7
The Red Ants

"Well?" said Jason the next day. We were in the garden at my house this time. I'd asked him to come over so that I could give his Truth Glasses back to him.

"Nothing. Not a thing. Not one damn thing."

"Why don't I believe you?"

"Why would I lie? I wore them for 15 minutes last night and all I got out of it was sore eyes."

"Then why do you want me to have them back so much?"

"Because my bedroom's already full of stuff and there's no space. Plus my mum's asked a few funny questions about them. I couldn't really tell her what they are, although when I told her *you* had made them she sort of went, 'Ah', in that way she has, you know. And she called you the Nutty Professor again."

"She does like that nickname. It's a shame *I* don't like it much."

"Hey, if my mum gives you a nickname, that means you're all right. Not all my friends get nicknames."

"You don't have that many other friends."

"Harsh, Jason."

"But fair. Listen, Dan, if you want to think you didn't see anything with the glasses, that's fine by me. I know what I saw anyway.

I think I'm on to something here. By the way, did I tell you I've found some more ants in the garden? Red ones this time."

"No."

"Want to come and have a look? Red ants are much more exciting than black ants. They can sting."

"I know. OK, I'll come."

We went through all the bit with the front door, making it seem as if we were going out that way. Then we crept back past my mum's office. She was busy tapping away at her computer. She wouldn't have noticed us anyway.

We tiptoed across the garden and pushed our way down the bank of the cutting. At the bottom I waited, as always, and did my careful left-and-right check. But Jason didn't bother. He seemed to think it was OK to skip straight across the railway tracks without even a glance either way.

I had a go at him when we'd got across to the other side. I told him he was being stupid. He really *had* to look before crossing the railway track. He'd kill himself one day if he didn't.

"Oh, I'll always be OK, Dan," he said. His voice went all dreamy again, like when he'd shown me the glasses. "I know when God's there and when He isn't. I know when He's looking. Right this moment He's turned away. He's not taking any notice of me, or of you."

"Is that so?" I said, and tried to laugh. I wanted to tell Jason he was starting to scare me. This Big Idea was starting to get out of control. He was believing things he shouldn't be believing.

But I didn't say anything. I couldn't find the right words and I didn't want to hurt Jason's feelings. He could be very sensitive. At school he sometimes burst into tears in class when he knew the answer to a question and had his hand up and the teacher didn't ask him. Then there were the times when he lost it, went crazy. Some of the older kids liked to take the piss out of him. They would call him nerd and loonie and freak show and lots of bad names. Jason could take it up to a point and then he would go psycho. He turned into a human whirlwind. He would attack the guys who were teasing him and kick out at them with his legs. Of course, the bullies found this funny so they tried to get at him whenever they had the chance. They hoped they'd get him to go psycho again.

I admired Jason because he did fight back sometimes, even if it never got him very far. Me, I always keep my head down if there's trouble. I never let the bullies get to me. I think I'm a bit of a coward. But Jason – push him hard enough and he was as blind-brave as a boy can be.

Anyway, that afternoon we stopped talking about God. We crept into Jason's

garden. We didn't go all the way in. The red
ants' nest was in the bit at the end that was
all overgrown and wild.

The ants' nest was in a broken-off, rotten
tree branch that was lying on the ground.
Jason pointed to all the tiny holes they'd
made. Then he showed me a bigger hole at
one end of the branch. The ants were
trooping in and out through the hole and on
to the ground in two parallel lines, much like
the black ants on the patio. They weren't
really red but a rather pale rust colour.

We watched them for a while, and then, of
course, Jason decided he couldn't leave them
alone. Before I could say anything he grabbed
a twig and began banging it down near the
two-way line of ants on the ground.

"I am your god!" he boomed, like God in
one those old films with lots of heroes and
shouting. "Kneel before me and worship me!
I hold the power of the mighty twig in my

hands! Your lives are mine to do with as I please!"

Until now the ants hadn't been bothered by the jabs of the twig. It wasn't coming close enough to disturb them. But now Jason moved the twig closer and started stabbing at the ants. Sure enough, he was soon squishing them to death with the twig's tip.

"Die! Die! Die because I have decreed it! I am your lord and master! You are nothing to me! Less than nothing! This is how I destroy you! This is how I end your useless lives!"

"Jason, that's enough," I said. "Leave it."

"Hear my voice, O tiny ants! Feel my anger! *You* must die!" He crushed one ant. "And *you*!" He crushed another. "There is no escape! Flee, flee all you like! I am God! You cannot run from *me*!"

"I mean it, Jason. Stop. You're being a prat."

"Your hour of doom has come! It's the end of the world! The final hour! Pray to me and I may show mercy!"

"Jason, you madman, that's enough."

I grabbed his arm. All I wanted to do was pull him away so that he couldn't kill any more ants with the twig.

Jason had bent down to look at the ants and when I grabbed him, he lost his balance.

Next thing I knew, he'd fallen over sideways. He tried to stop himself falling all the way by putting out one of his hands. The hand landed on the rotten branch. The rotten branch crumbled away. All at once, Jason's hand was covered in red ants. The ants were swarming all over it. It was like he had a glove on.

He started screaming and flapping his hand madly.

"They're biting me! Ow, Dan, they're biting me! Ow, it hurts! It hurts like hell!"

I was frozen. My mind had stopped dead. I didn't know what to do.

Then I moved. I grabbed Jason's arm and started slapping his hand to brush the ants off. Some of them got onto my hand and began biting me too. I ignored the pain, which felt like sharp needle jabs on my skin. I kept slapping at Jason's hand. I tried to clear the angry ants off as fast as I could.

Soon there were only a few left. Jason pulled his hand away and slapped at it. He killed the last few ants that still clung to him. I did the same with the ants on my hand. I didn't mind killing them now. They were hurting me. I had to stop them.

When all the ants that were attacking us were dead, we stood up slowly. We looked at our hands. Jason's was much worse than mine. There were hundreds of little red marks all over it. He was in real pain. His eyes glistened with tears.

We ran indoors and found Jason's mother. As soon as she heard what had happened, she rushed us up to the bathroom and took a small spray out of the cupboard. The stuff in the spray stopped the ant bites from stinging. She sprayed it all over our bitten hands, and we began to feel better. We both said it had been an accident. Jason had fallen over and stuck his hand in the ants' nest. I had got stung while I was helping him. This was almost the truth and Jason's mum believed us. She said we should be more careful, and that was that.

Later, I set off home. I nearly went the proper way, along the street and over the bridge. But, in the end, I decided to cross the tracks. I wanted to see what had happened to the red ants.

The rotten branch was now just a small pile of crumbled bits of wood. The ants had gone. There was not one left. They'd set off to find a new place to build a nest.

I found the Truth Glasses not far from the branch. We had left them there in all the panic.

I picked them up and took them home. I thought I'd give them to Jason next time we met.

I didn't know there wasn't going to be a next time.

Chapter 8

Jason's Message

Two days after the red ants' attack, Jason tried to ring me. My mobile was turned off so he left a message. I'd turned my mobile off because I was out with my mum and dad. We had gone to see my gran in the country. It was the last Saturday of the holidays. School was due to start again on the Monday.

The morning had started out hot and by midday it was boiling. My parents and my gran kept saying how hot it was. In fact, I think that's all they talked about. My gran's old and she says the same thing again and again.

As we were driving home, I turned my phone on and heard Jason's message.

The message said, "Dan, it's Jason. Look, even if you don't believe me about all this, I think we've screwed up. I think we've really screwed up. Those ants, what happened with them – it's shown me something. We have to be responsible. We have to think about other creatures. Gods have to be responsible, because they can get hurt. People can turn on them and hurt them. My hand's swollen up like a balloon. That's the proof. The ants turned on me when I was their god. People can scare gods just as much as gods can scare people.

"So I don't think we should look too hard into any of this stuff any more. The ants are better off not knowing about their gods. Same with us. We're better off not knowing about *our* gods. Do you understand me? There are some things we just mustn't mess with. Do you know what I'm saying?

"Have you got the Truth Glasses? I went looking for them yesterday. I left them at the end of the garden, didn't I? But you took them and you've got them. Right?

"Smash them, Dan. Maybe that'll help. Maybe that'll save us. Smash those Truth Glasses. Take a hammer to them and break them to bits. It might just work. We might just be all right then.

"OK, that's it. Call me back when you can.

"And take care, Dan. Look out. Be very, very careful."

"Who was that, Daniel?" said my mum. She turned round to look at me. I was sitting in the back of the car.

"Um, Jason."

"And what did the Nutty Professor want?"

"Not a lot. Nothing much. Just saying hi."

"Long message just to say hi. It went on for over a minute."

"You know Jason. He can talk. I'm going to call him back."

I tried to, but my mobile started playing up. I'd been able to hear Jason's message from the voicemail but I couldn't make a call. The phone said NO NETWORK and I couldn't get a signal.

I couldn't work out why. We were near the city. There shouldn't have been any problem with getting a signal.

I looked out of the car window and then I saw what the trouble was.

There were huge thunderclouds up ahead, over the city. They were thick and purple and nasty. It had been so hot that day, now we were going to have a storm. "Looks like we're driving into bad weather," said my dad.

Chapter 9

The Storm

My dad was right. Almost as soon as he'd said that, splashes of rain began hitting the car windscreen. All at once a torrent of water came down. My dad switched on the windscreen wipers and the headlights and slowed the car right down.

The rain crashed onto the road. It hammered on the car roof. Thunder roared and shook. It sounded as if it wasn't just in the sky but all around us. The whole world seemed to tremble with it. Flashes of lightning shot between the clouds, like sharp cracks of silver.

All the traffic on the road slowed to a crawl. We should have reached home by five at the latest. In the end, we didn't get there till after seven. Some streets were flooded. This caused some nasty tailbacks and traffic jams.

The storm went on and on. On the car radio the news said it was one of the worst storms people could remember. Nobody had seen it coming. The weathermen hadn't predicted it.

I had a very bad feeling about all of this. There was a knot of worry inside me, put there by Jason's message. It grew slowly bigger and bigger. By the time we got home, I felt really scared.

We dashed inside with our arms over our heads to keep off the rain. My mum went to get a towel for us to dry ourselves off with.

I went to the telephone and rang Jason's mobile. No good. I only got his voicemail. I tried his home number. His mother answered.

"Daniel? Yes, Jason's in. He's up in his room, I think. Isn't this storm awful? That's why you're not using your mobile. Do you want me to call him down?"

"Yes, I do, please, Mrs Finnegan."

Jason arrived at the phone a minute or so later.

"Dan, have you done it? Have you smashed them?"

"No, not yet. I haven't had a chance. I've only just got in."

"What are you waiting for? Do it. Do it now, before it's too late."

"Jason, do you really think—"

"I don't *think*, Dan, I *know*. I *know*. You have to smash them. Look, I'm coming over. I'll help you. My dad's got a big hammer in the shed. I'll grab that and be right over. OK? Meet me in your garden with the glasses."

"No, come round the front way, Jason."

"No time. Much quicker by the back."

"The front way, Jason." I don't know why it seemed important to me that he didn't cross the railway tracks. It just did.

I don't think he heard me say it that second time, though. He had already hung up.

I charged upstairs to get the Truth Glasses. When I came down, my mother wanted to know where I was going in such a hurry.

"To meet Jason," I said.

"Not now, you're not. In this weather? Are you mad?"

"I have to."

"No, you don't have to. It's dinner time. I'm making us something to eat. I've just taken some pizzas out of the oven. You're going to stay right here. It'll have to wait till tomorrow."

I held the glasses up. "He needs to have these back. Now."

"No, he doesn't. He can have them back tomorrow."

"*Please*, Mum."

"Daniel, I mean it. Put them down, dry your hair with this towel, then lay the table. Do something useful."

"No!"

It was fear more than anything that made me defy her. I wasn't being bold. I was scared.

Scared of what? I couldn't say. But somehow the storm outside told me there was plenty to be scared of.

I pushed past my mother. I burst out through the back door. At once, the rain was pounding down on my skull and the thunder was roaring in my ears. The lightning was dazzling me. I dimly heard my mother shout behind me, and then my father shout too. I ignored them and set off across the lawn. The ground was sodden under my feet. It felt like a swamp.

It was coming.

I didn't know what *it* was.

But I did know that whatever it was, it was huge and it was terrible.

I slipped and fell to my knees. I almost dropped the Truth Glasses. I got up and staggered on. I pushed my way through the bushes. I crashed into the fence. I squeezed through the gap. I wobbled at the top of the bank as I tried to look down between the thorn bushes. In spring the bushes had green leaves, but now the branches were brown and twisted, like claws. They were whipping about in the wind. I couldn't see a thing.

I started to go down the bank but I didn't get far. Brambles pulled at my clothes. Ivy tangled around my ankles and trapped me. I tried to get free but I was stuck.

I think I heard Jason calling out my name then.

I think he was shouting to me as he made his way onto the tracks.

I'm sure he was telling me that he was coming, that I should hold on, that everything was going to be all right.

Then there was a whooshing rumble.

Then there was the sound of screeching brakes.

The rain pelted down, and I stood there. I was held fast by the thorn bushes.

And I knew that Jason was dead.

I *knew*.

Chapter 10
The Thing

There isn't much more to add.

I don't really want to say any more.

I'll say just this.

In the moments after I heard the train, I was numb. I didn't have a thought in my head.

Except one.

Use the Truth Glasses.

They were there in my hand. They were there to be looked through.

They could show me the truth, if I dared to look.

Use the Truth Glasses.

I was trembling as I lifted them up to my face. I'd like to say it was the chill of my wet clothes that made me shiver like that. It wasn't.

I lifted the glasses up and I put them on.

I didn't want to look.

I *had* to look.

I left the glasses in place for just a few seconds, for just the shortest length of time, and then I pulled them off again.

In those seconds I saw something I wish I could forget and know I'll never forget.

It was gigantic, the size of a mountain. It walked like a man. It moved with a kind of shabby grace. Its arms and legs swung slowly like the parts of a huge machine. It was turning away from the railway line. It was turning its back on what it had done.

I think there was a smile on its moon-like face as it shambled off.

The smile stayed there for only a heartbeat and then vanished.

It was a smile of mischief and evil.

The *thing* knew it had done something bad. But it didn't care. It thought about its action the way you or I might think about slapping a gnat.

Or squashing a fly.

Or killing an ant.

Barrington Stoke would like to thank all its readers for commenting on the manuscript before publication and in particular:

Miss J Adams
Christopher Anderson
Daniel Appleby
Alison Bell
Catherine Brotherston
Marion Clark
Rachel Cooke
Jennifer Cotton
Cassie Cousins
Rhona Cunningham
Catherine Dodd
Vicky Drysdale
Hanna Dunn
Lisa-Marie Forge
Jack Girling
Gabriel Hills
Nadia Holmes
Sophie Hughes
Kristie Hyde
Oliver Jacob
Christine Johnson
Davina Kenny
Michael Kozma

Megan Lewis
McKenzie Lloyd-Smith
Gail Macleod
Kirsty McArthur
Eve McCowat
Adam Medley
Lucky Nwosu
Zoe Pattenden
Luke Pearson
Christina Ramsay
William Reddaway
Mrs R Richey
Kirsty Roberts
Natasha Robinson
James Salmond
David Sanders
Sherri Sawyer
Jason Stanforth
Catherine Stirling Hill
Amanda Wallace
Penny Ward
Sarah Wilkinson

Become a Consultant!

Would you like to give us feedback on our titles before they are published? Contact us at the email address below – we'd love to hear from you!

info@barringtonstoke.co.uk
www.barringtonstoke.co.uk

If you loved this book, why don't you read ...

Wings

by James Lovegrove

ISBN 1-842991-93-0

Az dreams of being like everyone else. In the world of the Airborn that means growing wings. It seems impossible, but with an inventor for a father, who knows?

You can order **Wings** directly from our website at
www.barringtonstoke.co.uk

If you loved this book, why don't you read ...

The House of Lazarus

by James Lovegrove

ISBN 1-842991-25-6

"What if you were able to stay in touch with your loved ones even after they had been taken from you?"

Joey's mum didn't want to die. So she made Joey promise to rent her a place at the House of Lazarus, where they say they can keep people alive for ever. It costs a lot to keep her there and Joey finds it hard to pay the rent. Then he has a strange dream and begins to wonder if he has done the right thing. Can the House of Lazarus really give people the gift of eternal life?

You can order *The House of Lazarus* directly from our website at **www.barringtonstoke.co.uk**